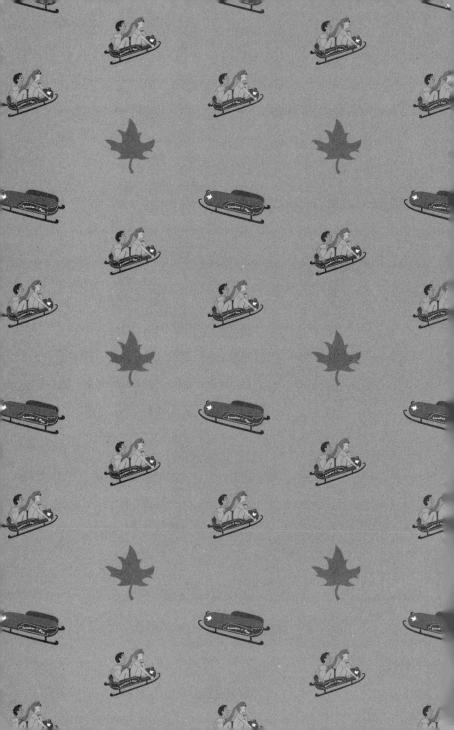

Teachers, librarians, and kids from across Canada are talking about the *Canadian Flyer Adventures.* Here's what some of them had to say:

I love the fact that these are Canadian adventures—kids should know how exciting Canadian history is. Emily and Matt are regular kids, full of curiosity, and I can see readers relating to them. ~ *JEAN K., TEACHER, ONTARIO*

What kids told us:

I would like to have the chance to ride on a magical sled and have adventures. ~ *EMMANUEL*

I would like to tell the author that her book is amazing, incredible, awesome, and a million times better than any book I've read. ~ *MARIA*

I would recommend the *Canadian Flyer Adventures* series to other kids so they could learn about Canada too. The book is just the right length and hard to put down. ~ *PAUL*

The books I usually read are the full-of-fact encyclopedias. This book is full of interesting ideas that simply grab me. ~ *ELEANOR*

At the end of the book Matt and Emily say they are going on another adventure. I'm very interested in where they are going next! ~ *ALEX*

I like when Emily and Matt fly into the sky on a sled towards a new adventure. I can't wait for the next book! ~ *JI SANG*

Far from Home

Frieda Wishinsky

Illustrated by Leanne Franson

MAPLE
TREE
PRESS

Maple Tree Press books are published by Owlkids Books Inc.
10 Lower Spadina Avenue, Suite 400, Toronto, Ontario M5V 2Z2
www.mapletreepress.com

Text © 2008 Frieda Wishinsky   Illustrations © 2008 Leanne Franson

Distributed in Canada by Raincoast Books
9050 Shaughnessy Street, Vancouver, British Columbia V6P 6E5

Distributed in the United States by Publishers Group West
1700 Fourth Street, Berkeley, California 94710

Dedication
For my niece, friend, and fellow author Rebecca O'Connell (Ben-Zvi)

Acknowledgements
Many thanks to the hard-working Maple Tree/Owlkids team, for their insightful comments
and steadfast support. Special thanks to Leanne Franson and Barb Kelly for their engaging
and energetic illustrations and design.

Cataloguing in Publication Data
Wishinsky, Frieda
Far from home / Frieda Wishinsky ; illustrated by Leanne Franson.

(Canadian flyer adventures ; 11)
ISBN 978-1-897349-42-7 (bound). ISBN 978-1-897349-43-4 (pbk.)

1. World War, 1939– 1945—Evacuation of civilians—Great Britain—Juvenile fiction.
2. World War, 1939– 1945—Children—Canada—Juvenile fiction.
I. Franson, Leanne II. Title. III. Series: Wishinsky, Frieda. Canadian flyer adventures ; 11.

PS8595.I834F37 2008   jC813'.54   C2008-902040-5

Library of Congress Control Number: 2008925713

Design & art direction: Barb Kelly
Illustrations: Leanne Franson

We acknowledge the financial support of the Canada Council   ONTARIO ARTS COUNCIL
for the Arts, the Ontario Arts Council, the Government   CONSEIL DES ARTS DE L'ONTARIO
of Canada through the Book Publishing Industry Development Program (BPIDP), and the
Government of Ontario through the Ontario Media Development Corporation's Book Initiative
for our publishing activities.

Printed in Canada
Ancient Forest Friendly: Printed on 100% Post-Consumer Recycled Paper

A   B   C   D   E   F

CONTENTS

HOW IT ALL BEGAN

Emily and Matt couldn't believe their luck. They discovered an old dresser full of strange objects in the tower of Emily's house. They also found a note from Emily's Great-Aunt Miranda: "The sled is yours. Fly it to wonderful adventures."

They found a sled right behind the dresser! When they sat on it, shimmery gold words appeared:

Rub the leaf
Three times fast.
Soon you'll fly
To the past.

The sled rose over Emily's house. It flew over their town of Glenwood. It sailed out of a cloud and into the past. Their adventures on the flying sled had begun! Where will the sled take them next? Turn the page to find out.

1

The Letter

"Look what just came in the mail!" Emily waved a letter. She raced down the front steps to meet Matt.

"Who's it from?" asked Matt.

"You won't believe it! You have to read it." Emily handed Matt the letter.

Matt read it aloud.

Dear Bing Family,

My name is Kate Norris. When we were children, my brother John and I were billeted with Miranda Bing and her parents in your house. It was in the 1940s, during World War II.

I'll be visiting Canada next month, and I wondered if I might stop by to see you and visit the house again? It would mean so much to me.

John recently told me that he'd hidden a locket in your house. Unfortunately, he can't recall exactly where he hid it. Our mother gave me the locket before we left England. Would you mind looking for it? I would be so grateful.

Best wishes,
Kate Norris

"Wow!" said Matt. "Let's look for the locket right now. It would be awesome if we found it!"

"And it would be awesome to meet Kate Norris," said Emily. "Let me think...if she

2

was a kid in the 1940s, she'd probably be in her seventies now, like Great-Aunt Miranda. We'll have to ask Ms. Norris what Great-Aunt Miranda was like back then."

"I wonder why John hid the locket," said Matt. "I bet he and his sister had a fight. I once hid my Cousin Maria's stuffed pig after she knocked down my block castle."

"So, where would an angry kid hide a locket?" asked Emily.

"How about the tower room?"

Emily's eyes lit up. "Of course! The locket might even be inside the dresser."

Emily and Matt zoomed up the rickety stairs to the tower room. As soon as they were inside, Emily popped open the top drawer of the dresser and peered in. "I don't see a locket here."

"Look in the corner," said Matt. "I see a

label that says *Glenwood, Ontario, 1940*. It's attached to something, but I can't see what."

Emily pulled the label out. It was stapled to a small envelope. "It's addressed to Mr. and Mrs. Norris, but there's no stamp."

"Is there a letter inside?" asked Matt.

Emily reached inside the envelope. A thin, yellowing piece of paper fluttered to the floor. She picked it up. "Wow! It's from Kate to her mom!" she said. "Listen!"

Dear Mummy,   *September 15, 1940*

John and I miss you so much! The Bings are nice, but we want to go home. We're so worried about everyone. We haven't heard anything from you in two weeks, and the newspapers are full of reports of bombing in London.

Please...

"Please what?" asked Matt.

"I don't know. That's where the letter ends. Kate never finished it."

"I wonder what happened to Kate and John back then. And I wonder what your Great-Aunt Miranda was like as a kid—and what Glenwood and your house looked like in those days."

"There's only one way to find out," said Emily.

Matt grinned. "So, what are we waiting for? I have my recorder. Do you have your sketchbook?

"Right here in my pocket."

"Then let's fly, Em!"

2

Where Is He?

Emily pulled the sled out from behind the dresser. The two friends hopped on.

As soon as they did, shimmery words appeared.

Rub the leaf
Three times fast.
Soon you'll fly
To the past.

Immediately, the sled was covered in fog.

When it lifted, they soared over Emily's house, over Glenwood, and into a fluffy white cloud.

When the sled burst out of the cloud, they were flying over an ocean.

"Yikes!" said Emily. "We're not going to Glenwood in 1940. We're heading down toward the ocean!"

"I just hope we don't land *in* the ocean."

The sled flew lower and then veered toward a large ship in a harbour.

"Phew! It looks like we're going to end up on that ship, not in the water," said Matt.

"Hold on tight. We're about to hit the deck!"

With a *kerplunk*, the sled landed.

Emily and Matt jumped off the sled. They looked around, but there was no one in sight.

"Now what are we supposed to do?" asked Emily.

"Find someone or get off the ship," said Matt.

Matt and Emily pulled the sled and walked around the wooden deck. It was lined with chairs, but no one was sitting in any of them.

"It's like a ghost ship," said Emily.

And then they heard a girl's voice. "Where are you? We have to get off the ship! Now!"

A door on the deck sprung open. A girl of about nine, wearing a navy blue dress, charged out. Her straight brown hair was clipped to one side. It bounced up and down as she raced along the deck.

Emily and Matt hurried after her. "Wait!" they called out.

The girl spun around. "Oh, I'm glad someone's still on the ship. Have you seen a little boy with a one-eared stuffed rabbit?"

"We haven't seen anyone," said Matt.

"Who's the boy?" Emily asked.

"My brother. He cried all the way across the Atlantic, and now he refuses to talk to me or to anyone. I promised Mum that I'd take care of him, and now I can't find him anywhere."

"We'll help you look," said Emily. "What's his name?"

"John. And my name is Kate."

Matt and Emily stared at each other. The girl had to be Kate Norris! But what was she doing with her brother on a ship instead of in Glenwood?

3

The Locket

"My name is Emily, and this is Matt."

"Why don't we look in the cabins for your brother," suggested Matt.

They followed Kate down a long hall. "Why do you have a sled?" she asked.

"There's lots of snow in Canada, and it's fun to take sled rides," said Matt.

Kate sighed. "I'd love to ride a sled down a snowy hill. I've never done that before. I guess we'll have to wait a few months for that to happen."

Emily and Matt nodded. It was still warm out. It was hard to think of snow.

Matt left the sled beside a lifeboat. Then they ran from cabin to cabin and opened each door. They called John's name, but they didn't see or hear anyone.

They followed Kate to the dining room, but it was also empty. They searched the crew's quarters, but no one was there either. They poked inside all the lifeboats, but there was no one anywhere on the ship.

"He couldn't just disappear," said Kate as they circled the deck once more. "What if I never find him? What if he—?" Kate gulped and glanced over the ship's railing into the ocean.

Emily patted Kate on the shoulder. "I'm sure he didn't fall into...anything," she said. "He has to be here somewhere. We'll find him."

"But we've looked everywhere. He's gone. Mum will never forgive me." Kate reached for a heart-shaped silver locket that hung around her neck.

Emily and Matt glanced at each other. That had to be the locket Kate wrote about in her letter!

"We haven't looked everywhere!" said Matt. He ran over to a deck chair. It was covered with a pile of red and blue blankets. "There's something lumpy under these blankets."

Matt pulled the blankets off. A curly-haired boy in short pants and a buttoned-up jacket was asleep underneath. He was clutching a one-eared, ragged rabbit.

Kate raced over. "John!" she said, shaking the sleeping boy. "I've been so worried about you. Wake up. We have to get off the ship. Now!"

John opened his big brown eyes and then closed them. He held his rabbit tighter and pulled the blankets back over his head.

Kate yanked the blankets off. She grabbed her brother's arm and pulled, but John wouldn't budge.

He kicked his sister in the shins.

"Ouch! Stop!" cried Kate.

"Come on, John," said Matt. "You have to get up. We all have to get off the ship."

But John wouldn't move.

"Now what?" groaned Kate.

4

Are You Sure?

"I have an idea," Emily whispered to Kate.

"Want a ride on the sled, John?" Emily asked the small boy.

John poked his head out from under the blankets, but he didn't say anything or move from the chair.

"We can make it go fast," said Matt.

John thrust his head out farther, but he still didn't get off the chair.

"You have to come with us right now, or no ride," said Emily.

John looked at Emily. Then he tossed the blankets off and plunked himself down on the sled.

"Okay, here we go," she said. Emily pulled John till they reached the end of the ship's deck. "You have to climb off now," she said. "We can't pull it up the gangway."

John slid off the sled. Matt carried the sled up the gangway and into a red brick building.

When they were on a flat surface again, John tugged at Matt's sleeve. He pointed to the sled.

"Okay. One more ride," said Matt.

John sat down on the sled.

"I said we'd go fast, so here we go! Ready?" said Matt.

John nodded.

Matt raced the sled along for a way. "Now, hop off. It's getting too crowded."

John slid off the sled. Matt, Emily, and Kate headed farther into the building, but John didn't move.

"Please keep going," Kate pleaded with her brother. John stuck his tongue out at his sister, but he followed her through the building.

It was buzzing with children and officials.

A woman in a brown suit walked around speaking to children and ticking names off in a large notebook. She approached Kate, John, Emily, and Matt.

"Welcome to Halifax, children. I'm Mrs. King from the Overseas Reception Board," she said. "What are your names?"

"I'm Kate Norris, and this is my brother, John," said Kate.

Mrs. King looked down her list. "Yes. I see your names. You're staying with the Bings in Glenwood, Ontario. The train leaves in two hours. Your suitcases are over there. Mrs. Gold will be on your train to accompany you and make sure you arrive in Glenwood safely."

While Kate and John headed off to find their suitcases, Mrs. King turned to Emily and Matt. "What are your names?" she asked.

"I'm Matt Martinez, and this is Emily Bing."

Mrs. King checked her list. "I don't see your names on my list."

"We're supposed to stay with the Bings, too. They're my relatives," said Emily.

"I see," said Mrs. King, checking her list again. "But your names are not here. This is most unusual. Wait here."

"Oh no!" said Emily. "What if she doesn't let us go to Glenwood?"

5

This Is Magic!

"Here she comes!" said Matt.

"Well, children," said Mrs. King, "we have decided that since Emily is related to the Bings, you will join Kate and John Norris. It is irregular, but in wartime, exceptions must be made. I wish you a safe journey." Mrs. King wrote their names on her list and marched off to help other children.

"Phew!" said Matt. "Now all we have to do is explain to Miranda and her parents who we are."

"Yikes!" said Emily. "I don't know what we're going to tell them."

"We'll think of something," Matt reassured her. "We have three days on the train to think."

"But we don't have any suitcases. People will think that's weird. I don't want to wear this skirt and blouse the whole time. It's hot, and it's going to get stinky." Emily looked down at her red plaid skirt and white shirt, and then at Matt's short black pants and white shirt.

"I know, but at least we're going to Glenwood, and we'll meet your Great-Aunt Miranda! That's awesome! Let's tell Kate and John we're travelling with them."

Emily and Matt scurried over to the side of the building, where Kate and John were still searching for their suitcases.

"I've found mine but not John's," said Kate.

"This is my day for losing things. First my brother and now his suitcase! I'm glad I haven't lost my locket."

Kate showed them the picture of her family inside the locket. "Mum gave this to me the day we left London. She promised we'd all be 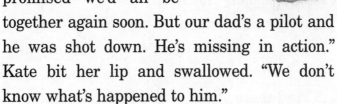 together again soon. But our dad's a pilot and he was shot down. He's missing in action." Kate bit her lip and swallowed. "We don't know what's happened to him."

"That's hard," said Emily. She could tell that Kate was trying not to cry.

"I'm sure you'll see your family one day soon," said Matt. "We're staying in Glenwood with the Bings, too! Emily's related to them."

Kate's face broke into a smile. "That's terrific.

It will be fun playing together. I hope their daughter Miranda is nice. Have you ever met her, Emily?"

"No," said Emily, "but I've heard lots about her. I know she likes adventures."

"I like adventures, too," said Kate. "Have you found your suitcases yet?"

"No," said Emily. "They're probably lost."

"Look! This must be yours," said Kate, pointing to a suitcase. "It says *Emily Bing*."

Emily stared at the small leather suitcase. "That's amazing," she said. "It *is* mine."

"And there's mine," said Matt, walking over to a suitcase leaning against Emily's. It had a label with his name on it. "This *is* magic."

Kate laughed. "I could use a little magic to find John's case."

"Is this it?" said Emily, pointing to a battered suitcase that had been tossed in a corner.

"Hurrah. You found it!" exclaimed Kate. "You two are the best at finding brothers and suitcases!"

"I know," said Emily, winking at Matt. "We've got the magic!"

"Come on," said Kate. "We'd better head to the train station. It's right inside the building, but our train leaves soon."

"Which lady is Mrs. Gold?" asked Matt. "She's supposed to look out for us on the train."

"She's the lady with the red suit and red hat," said Kate. "She got angry with John on the ship when he didn't answer her. When I told her he hasn't spoken to anyone because he's worried about our family, she said, 'All the children on this ship are worried. That's no excuse to be rude.'"

6

Cowboys or Kangaroos?

An hour later they were boarding the train with ten other children from the ship. Mrs. Gold had given them each labels with their names on them to wear around their necks.

"I do not want anyone to take this label off," she said in a clipped voice. "And you are not to leave the train at any time. You have been entrusted to my care, and I want to ensure you arrive safely at your destination. Understood?"

"Yes, Mrs. Gold," said the children.

"She's so bossy," Emily whispered to Matt.

"She sounds like a general in the army," Matt whispered back.

"Look at these bunk beds," said Kate, when they were inside the train's sleeping car. "I want to sleep on top."

"I want the top, too," said Emily.

"I'll take the bottom," said Matt.

John flopped down on the other bottom bunk, beneath Kate.

"Good. That's all settled," said Kate. "See, this is going to be an adventure, John. You'll like Glenwood, and Emily and Matt will be with us. Isn't that terrific?"

John shook his head no.

"Come on, John," said Matt. "We really will have fun. Cheer up."

John shook his head harder.

"Oh, forget about him," said Kate. "I'm tired

of trying to cheer him up all the time. I'm worried about Dad, too, but I'm still speaking. If John wants to be Mr. Grumpy, he can. The train is starting to move. Come on! Let's look out the window."

The children ran to the window and watched the train pull out of the station. It passed warehouses, shops, and homes. Then it headed toward the Nova Scotia countryside. Soon they could see sparkling lakes, rolling farm country, and dense forests.

"Mum asked what John and I preferred: cowboys or kangaroos," said Kate. "*Cowboys* meant we'd be evacuated to Canada, and *kangaroos* meant we'd go to Australia. I wanted to see kangaroos, but John screamed that he wanted cowboys, or he wasn't going anywhere."

"I don't think there are a lot of cowboys in Ontario," said Matt.

"I know. But we only found that out on the second day at sea, and you should have heard John bellow. The next night we had a lifeboat drill. John refused to get into the lifeboat. He screamed that he didn't want to die like Dad. I told him Dad wasn't dead, just missing, but he just kept yelling and yelling. The next morning he stopped speaking. Now he just shakes his head, nods, and points." Kate sighed. "How can I explain that to the Bings? What if John never talks to anyone again?"

"I'm sure he'll talk soon," said Emily. She glanced at Matt. She knew he was thinking the same thing she was. The Bings would understand about a frightened little boy but what would they say about Emily and Matt? How could they explain who *they* were?

"Don't worry. We'll think of something," Matt whispered to Emily.

"We'd better," said Emily in a low voice. For the next three days, the train zipped past cornfields, forests, and farmhouses. Emily drew  pictures in her sketchbook of deer nibbling grass at the edge of the forest and cows grazing in fields.

Emily, Matt, and Kate played checkers and cards. John spent hours staring silently out the window.

"What will your hosts say about such ridiculous behaviour?" Mrs. Gold chided John, wagging her finger. But her words made no difference. John wouldn't speak. Not to her. Not to anyone.

7

Great-Aunt Miranda?

"Glenwood! Next stop!" called the conductor.

"Come on, John," said Kate, grabbing her brother's hand. "This is it. You'd better talk now or else."

John shook his head and stuck his tongue out at Kate.

"Or else what?" whispered Matt to Kate.

"I don't know," said Kate in a low voice. "I just keep hoping something will make him talk."

The train ground to a halt.

"Emily, Matt, Kate, and John. Come with me," said Mrs. Gold.

The children grabbed their cases off the wooden shelves and followed Mrs. Gold off the train.

A short woman with curly brown hair stood beside a tall man and a girl of about ten. The girl was tall and skinny. Her sky blue eyes sparkled behind her glasses, and a mop of red hair curled around her face. Emily and Matt stared. There, right in front of them, stood Great-Aunt Miranda.

"I can't believe she's a kid like us," Emily whispered to Matt.

"There they are!" Miranda squealed, running toward the four children.

She thrust her hand forward. "Hi!" she said, shaking Kate's hand. "I'm Miranda Bing. You must be Kate, and that must be John...but who are you two?" She peered at Matt and Emily over her glasses. "Mom! Dad!" she called to her parents as they approached the group. "Are we supposed to have two more kids stay with us?"

"I don't think so," said Mrs. Bing.

"Emily Bing and Matt Martinez told me they've been assigned to stay with your family," said Mrs. Gold.

Emily glanced at Matt. Oh no! What should they say now? They'd forgotten to come up with a plan on the train.

"Is your last name really Bing like ours?" asked Miranda.

Emily took a deep breath. "Yes. I'm pretty sure I'm related to your family. Matt is my best friend, and we hope you'll let us stay because—"

"We have nowhere else to go," Matt chimed in.

Mrs. Bing looked at Mr. Bing. "Well...," she said.

"Please, Mom," said Miranda. "Let them stay. It will be fun having four new friends to play with at home. Emily could be our relative, and she and Matt have nowhere else to go." Miranda looked pleadingly at her parents.

"Well, it *is* wartime," said Mr. Bing. "And we want to do our part to help, so..."

Mrs. Bing smiled. "We'd be glad to have all four of you children stay with us. I'd be surprised if we were related, Emily. I don't think we have any family in England."

"Maybe we're distant relatives," said Emily. "Thanks for letting us stay."

Matt grinned. Emily was right. She was a distant relative—a relative from the future.

8

Bad News

"I love sleds!" said Miranda. "I'm getting a sled for my birthday in December. I bet your sled was made in Canada. It says *Canadian Flyer*. I'm glad you brought it. We're going to have so much fun flying down snowy hills together."

Emily grinned. "We love flying our sled."

"Every time we fly, it's an adventure," said Matt, winking at Emily.

They waited to see if Miranda would say anything more about flying or adventures, but she didn't.

"Do you have a sled?" she asked Kate.

"No, but I wish I had one." Kate and Miranda walked ahead together. Emily and Matt followed behind them. All the Bings helped the children carry their cases.

John trailed at the back with Mr. and Mrs. Bing. They asked him about the ship and his rabbit, but he just nodded his head yes or no.

"You must be tired," Mrs. Bing said to John, patting him on the back. "I bet you'd like a nice cup of cocoa."

Emily turned and saw John nod his head yes. He smiled for the first time that morning.

"We're almost there. Seeing the house is going to be amazing," Matt said to Emily.

"I have butterflies in my stomach just thinking about it," said Emily.

The two friends looked around Glenwood. It was different from the town they lived in.

There were fewer houses and stores, and, of course, no modern houses. People on the street smiled and waved hello to them.

Miranda was speaking so loudly that Emily and Matt could hear every word.

"You and Emily will sleep in my room. We have an extra bed in there, but nothing for Emily. We'll have to figure *something* out. Matt and your brother will sleep in the spare room. Why doesn't your brother talk? Is he sick?"

"No," muttered Kate. "He's just homesick. He's also worried about our dad. He's a pilot and he's missing in action."

"That's terrible," said Miranda. "When I went to camp last year, I was *so* homesick I cried for a whole day. But then I met everyone at camp, and I had *so* much fun I never wanted to go home. I bet John will have so much fun here, he'll forget about being worried."

"It's hard to forget," said Kate, fingering her locket. "I miss our mum and dad, too."

"You'll see. You'll love Glenwood. Everyone is friendly. And we have a tower room in our house that's like a castle. It's my favourite room. Sometimes I think there's magic up there."

Emily and Matt glanced at each other. What did Miranda mean about magic in the tower room?

"Here we are!" said Miranda.

"It's a nice house," said Kate politely, but she looked like she was going to cry.

"She looks really sad," Emily whispered to Matt.

"Miranda will cheer her up," said Matt. "She'd cheer anyone up! Look! Your house looks the same, except for the furniture."

"Come on! I want to show you my room,"

said Miranda. "I painted it yellow and green myself. Mom and Dad thought it would look strange, but I begged for a week and they finally agreed. I don't think it's strange. I think it's gorgeous."

Emily and Matt followed Miranda to her room.

It was Emily's room! But it looked totally different. One wall was yellow, another green, and two were half yellow and green. The quilt on Miranda's bed was half yellow and half green. And her walls were covered with photographs of famous places from all over the world, like the Eiffel Tower in Paris and the pyramids in Egypt.

"I'm going to visit all those places one day," said Miranda.

"I'd like to travel to those places, too," said Emily.

"You never know; we both might," said Miranda, winking at Emily. Emily glanced at Matt. Was Miranda hinting that she knew they came from the future?

But Miranda said nothing more about travelling or adventures. She showed them where they could put their clothes and where they'd sleep. Neighbours were bringing over a bed for Emily.

Matt was sharing a room with John. It had a desk and was lined with books. It looked like it had been a den before they changed it into a bedroom. The Bings were going to borrow a mattress from the neighbours for Matt, too. Matt shoved his suitcase and the sled into the closet.

After a supper of roast beef, potatoes, and salad, Mrs. Bing poured each child a big glass of milk. She added a dollop of ice cream.

"This is so good," said Kate. "We haven't had ice cream at home for a long time. We haven't had much butter or meat or sugar either since the war."

John slurped the ice cream and milk to the last drop, but he didn't say anything.

"Bedtime!" said Mrs. Bing when the children had finished dessert. "It's been a long day."

9

Where Did They Go?

The next morning, Mr. Bing turned the radio on after breakfast, to catch the latest war news.

"London has again suffered heavy casualties as the Germans continue to bomb the city," said the announcer. "Many people have been killed or injured. And we have just received news that more of our brave airmen have been shot down fighting the Germans."

Emily glanced at Kate. She was gulping back tears. John was clutching his rabbit. Then he turned and raced out of the room.

"Oh dear. He's upset hearing the news on the radio. Where's he going? Should we check on him?" asked Mrs. Bing.

"He'll be all right. It's just that we haven't heard from our mum since we left London," said Kate.

Mr. Bing patted Kate on the arm. "I wish there had been a letter waiting for you here. The mail is slow to arrive from overseas with the war in Europe. I'm sure you'll hear from your family soon. Try not to worry."

"I know what we should do!" said Miranda. She jumped up. "Let's play hide-and-seek. We can look for John first, and when we find him, we can make him look for one of us. I bet he'll like that!"

"I guess so," said Kate, but Emily and Matt could tell that Kate wasn't keen to play hide-and-seek.

But Miranda was. "Come on. Let's go find John!" she called.

"Great-Aunt Miranda is pretty bossy," Emily whispered to Matt.

"She's just trying to cheer everybody up," said Matt in a low voice.

The three children followed Miranda down the hall to the bedroom that John shared with Matt.

They checked in the beds and under the beds. No John. They checked the closet and under the desk. John wasn't there.

They looked in all the closets in the house, through the basement, and in the shed in the back garden. John wasn't anywhere.

"Where is he?" cried Kate. "Why does he keep running away?"

She sat down on a tree stump, put her head in her hands, and sobbed.

Emily put her arms around Kate. "Don't worry. We'll find him."

"And when we do," said Miranda, "I'm going to tell him that it's mean to make everyone worry, and it's silly not to talk to anybody."

Kate looked up and glared at Miranda.

"You don't understand. It's not silly. John is scared. So am I. Our house may have been bombed. Our dad may be dead. This war is so horrible!"

Kate stood up and stomped off toward the house.

"Oh no!" said Miranda. "I didn't mean to upset her."

"Let's go inside and talk to her," said Matt.

"Let's find John, too, but where could he be?" said Miranda. "We've looked everywhere."

"We haven't looked in the tower room," suggested Emily.

"You're right!" said Miranda.

The three children raced inside. They took a quick look in Miranda's bedroom for Kate, but she wasn't there.

They passed the kitchen where Miranda's parents were drinking coffee.

"Have you seen Kate?" Miranda asked.

"Don't tell me she's missing, too," said Miranda's mom.

"Don't worry, Mom. We'll find them both."

"I *am* worried. These children were put in our care, and now they're missing."

"They're here somewhere," said Miranda.

Matt and Emily followed Miranda up the rickety stairs to the tower room.

"This is so weird," Emily whispered to Matt. "We're going to the tower with my great-aunt, who's ten."

"And she says there might be magic there. What does she know? What does she mean?"

10

Promise Me

Miranda pushed the tower door open and laughed. "See? This room *is* magic. Look who it brought here!"

John was curled up and sound asleep on Emily and Matt's sled. He was clutching his one-eared rabbit.

"He must have carried the sled upstairs from our bedroom," said Matt.

"He likes our sled," said Emily.

"I like it, too!" said Miranda. "I can't wait to get my own sled. Now where's Kate?"

"Here I am," said Kate, opening the tower room door. "John! You're here!" she said.

She ran over to her brother. As she put her arms around him, he opened his eyes. "We've looked everywhere for you. You can't run away again. Promise me you won't."

John looked up at Kate but said nothing.

"Promise me," Kate insisted.

John nodded yes. He leaned his head against Kate.

"I'm sorry about what I said before," Miranda told Kate.

"It's all right. I was upset. I miss my parents," said Kate. "And the last few months have been so hard at home. We had to practise wearing these horrible gas masks and run to shelters in case the Germans bombed London. And now they have, and Dad is missing, and—"

Before Kate could finish, Mrs. Bing hurried

into the room. "Kate, I have something for you," she said. "A letter just arrived from England." She handed Kate the letter.

Kate gulped. Her hands trembled as she ripped the letter open.

Everyone waited as she read it.

"Mum is fine!" Kate exclaimed. "And Dad is alive! He's been hurt and he's in a hospital in France, but he's going to come home! Mum says our neighbourhood was bombed, but only the roof of our house was damaged."

Mrs. Bing hugged Kate, "We're so glad your family is safe. That's terrific news about your father."

"I know," said Kate. Then she began to cry. She dabbed the tears away with the back of her hand. "I'm sorry. It's just that I was so worried and now..."

John tugged at the sleeve of her blouse. "I want to see Mummy and Daddy," he muttered.

Kate gasped. "John, you're talking!" she exclaimed. She hugged her little brother.

"I want to see Dad NOW," sobbed John, burying his head in his sister's arm. "I want to go home."

"I understand," said Mrs. Bing. She patted John gently on the shoulder.

"No, you don't!" John screamed. He pushed her hand away. "I don't want to stay here any more." Tears rolled down his cheeks.

"John, that's rude," said Kate. "Mr. and Mrs. Bing and Miranda have been kind to us. It's not safe at home. Mum and Dad want us to stay here. That's what Mum wrote in her letter."

"I don't care. I'm not staying here. I hate it here."

Kate's face turned red. "Stop it, John. You're acting like a baby."

"I am not a baby," said John. "I hate you! I hate you!"

And he ran out of the tower room.

11

Follow Him

"I'm not chasing him this time," said Kate.

"He'll be fine," said Miranda. "Let's go outside and play in my yard."

"Go on, children," said Mrs. Bing. "I'll check on John in a bit. At least he's speaking. That's a good start."

Kate, Emily, and Matt followed Miranda to the backyard. Miranda sat on a black tire that hung between two trees.

"Look how high this can go," she said, pumping the tire with her feet. "Everyone can have a turn, and then I'll show you my secret garden." Miranda pointed to a narrow path between two huge maple trees.

"I love secret gardens," said Kate.

"Me, too," said Emily. "I want to draw a picture of it." Emily rummaged through the pockets of her skirt. "Where's my sketchbook? I had it this morning."

"Maybe you left it in the tower room," said Matt.

"I bet that's where it is. I'm going to get it before I see the garden."

"Just walk between the trees, and you'll be there," said Miranda.

"I'll help you look for your sketchbook," said Matt.

Emily and Matt ran into the house. "I want to take another look in the tower room," said Matt as they headed for the stairs. "Miranda keeps hinting there's magic. Maybe there's something magical there besides our sled."

But before they reached the tower room, they saw John hurrying toward the basement. At the door, he stopped and took something shiny out of his pocket. He wrapped it in a handkerchief and put it back in his pocket. Then he opened the basement door.

"I think he has Kate's locket in his pocket!" said Matt. "I bet he's going to hide it right now."

"Let's follow him," whispered Emily.

Emily and Matt opened the basement door quietly. They tiptoed down the stairs.

They watched John peer around the room. Then he ran over to a wall and pulled out a loose brick. He put the locket in the space and replaced the brick.

"He's going back up. *Run*," said Emily in a low voice.

"Let's head for the tower room," said Matt.

Emily and Matt dashed up the rickety stairs. Emily opened the door. "Phew! There's my sketchbook on the sled," she said.

"And there are words forming on the front of the sled!" said Matt.

He read the words aloud.

You made new friends.
You helped them too.
Now sit right down.
It's time you flew.

"I don't want to go home yet!" said Emily. "There's so much more I want to know about Miranda. And I want to see her secret garden. There's no secret garden in our yard in the future."

"But, Em, we have to go when the sled tells us. There's no time left. We can't even tell Kate about the locket. Well, not till we get back!"

"I have to write a note so no one will worry about us." Emily ripped a page out of her sketchbook and wrote:

Dear Mr. and Mrs. Bing, Miranda, Kate, and John,

We just heard we have to leave immediately for another town. We're going to stay with a different family.

Thanks for being so nice to us!

Emily and Matt

12

Home

Emily put the note on top of the dresser. Then she and Matt hopped on the sled. The sled rose immediately.

"Oh no!" said Matt. "I forgot to record anything about our adventure." He flipped on the recorder as the sled sailed over Glenwood. "Ladies and gentlemen, we have had an amazing adventure in Glenwood with Emily's Great-Aunt Miranda, except that it was Glenwood in 1940, and Miranda was only ten when we met her."

"We're heading into the cloud!" said Emily.

"Signing off!" Matt snapped the recorder off.

Soon they were back in the tower room in their own time.

They slid off the sled.

"I wonder if Kate will remember that she met two kids named Emily and Matt when she lived in Canada," said Emily.

"We were only around for a little while. But if she does, she'll probably think it's a coincidence that those kids had the same names as us. She'll never believe that she met us back then!" said Matt.

"The only person who might believe us is Great-Aunt Miranda, but she's far away in Paris," said Emily. Emily went to the dresser drawer and pulled out the picture of her aunt as a young girl.

"Matt! Look at this picture!" she shouted.

Matt stared at the picture of Miranda sitting on the sled. "Wow!" he said. "Miranda is—"

"Winking! She wasn't doing that before. Something has changed in the picture since we first looked at it. It's as if..."

"Miranda knew all about the magic, even then," said Matt. "Come on! Let's run down to the basement and see if the locket is still there."

The friends zoomed downstairs. "Do you remember which brick John hid the locket behind?" asked Emily.

"Sort of," said Matt, tapping and pulling at a brick.

They tapped and pulled at ten bricks, but none of them budged. Finally, the eleventh brick did.

"Yahoo! This has to be it!" said Matt. He slid the brick out and placed it on the ground. Then he felt inside the space. "I think...I think..."

"What? What?"

"I have it!" said Matt, pulling a rumpled handkerchief out. Matt unfolded the handker-chief, and inside lay Kate's locket. The silver had turned black, but the pictures of Kate, John, and their parents were still clear. "This is awesome. And there's more..."

Matt pulled out a little folded note from the space. He read it aloud.

Dear Kate,

I am not a big baby.

> *Your brother,*
> *John*

"Kate will be so happy we found the locket," said Emily. "Come on, Matt. Let's celebrate with some special Glenwood-in-the-old-days cookies."

"What are they?"

"A little dust, a little flour, some sugar, and a whole lot of magic!"

MORE ABOUT...

After their adventure, Matt and Emily wanted to know more about the Second World War and evacuated children. Turn the page for their favourite facts.

Matt's Top Ten Facts

1. World War II began on September 3rd, 1939, when Britain and France declared war on Germany. Canada declared war on Germany one week later.

> My grandfather said he'd never forget the day the war started.
> —E.

2. The United States declared war on Japan and Germany in December 1941, after the Japanese attacked Pearl Harbor, Hawaii.

3. Even before the war broke out, people in Britain thought their kids would be safer in the country and talked about sending them out of the big cities.

4. It wasn't until June 1940, when France fell to the German army, that many British kids were actually sent to the countryside for safety.

5. Many people worried that their kids wouldn't be safe even in the countryside, so they began sending

them to other countries. Many parents got in touch with relatives and friends abroad. But not everyone had the money to send their kids to other countries or knew people overseas.

6. Some British people said that those who evacuated their kids to other countries were cowards. Even the Prime Minister of Britain, Winston Churchill, said he didn't want the Germans to think that the British were scared.

7. When the Germans started to bomb British cities on September 7, 1940, people realized that the Germans were trying to scare people of all ages.

8. The German air force's (the Luftwaffe) bombing of British cities was called the Blitz.

9. On the first day of bombing, more than 430 people were killed and many more were injured.

10. The Germans bombed British cities almost every night to scare the people even more.

Emily's Top Ten Facts

It was a BIG, scary sleepover! —M.

1. People in London ran to underground shelters for safety during the Blitz. They often slept there.

2. The government in Britain tried to confuse the Luftwaffe about where people lived with blackouts at night. Street lamps were switched off, and black curtains hung in peoples' windows.

3. The bombing slowed down after May 1941, because the Germans had started to attack the Soviet Union.

4. Even though the bombing slowed down, by the end of the Blitz, 60,000 people had died, 87,000 had been badly injured, and two million homes had been destroyed.

5. The government program for sending kids overseas was called CORB (Children's Overseas Reception Board). It was created in May 1940, and was swamped with applications when the Blitz began.

6. CORB paid the travel costs and living expenses, so more people could send their kids to safety.

7. Lots of people in Canada, Australia, New Zealand, and South Africa volunteered to host kids from Britain. CORB matched kids with host families.

8. During the war, children who were sent to stay with families overseas were called Guest Children.

9. Long-distance telephone calls were expensive in the 1940s. Some radio stations let Guest Children speak to their parents over the radio, but most kids could only get in touch with their families by letter.

10. British people could only purchase limited amounts of food during the war, and had to use a special ration book, which kept track of what they were buying.

So You Want to Know...
FROM AUTHOR FRIEDA WISHINSKY

When I was writing this book, my friends wanted to know more about the Guest Children and their evacuation from Britain to Canada during World War II. I told them that all the characters in *Far From Home* were made up, but the story was based on historical facts. Here are some other questions I answered about those difficult times:

How many children were actually evacuated to Canada?

Although there were over 20,000 applications, in the end only about 3,000 children were evacuated through CORB. Starting in June 1940, children were sent to countries that had strong ties to Britain, such as Canada, Australia, New Zealand, and South Africa. About 1,500 children went to Canada through CORB. About 11,000 children went to these countries through other private arrangements.

What was the journey like across the Atlantic?

The ships carrying the children left from Liverpool and Greenock, near Glasgow, Scotland. To keep the passengers safe, the British government made sure that ships travelled as part of a convoy, or group of ships. But it was still very dangerous. The worst attacks came from German U-boats (submarines), which were hard to detect in those days. The U-boats would suddenly appear and try to torpedo the ships.

Did any of the ships carrying children actually get torpedoed?

On August 30th, 1940, a ship called *Volendam*, which carried about 300 CORB children, was torpedoed by a German U-boat and almost sunk. Luckily no one was killed or injured except for one of the crew who fell overboard and drowned. As soon as the torpedo hit, lifeboats were lowered into the water and the passengers were quickly transferred to other ships. The passengers returned to Scotland. Unfortunately soon after, on September 17, 1940, another ship carrying CORB children was really sunk.

What happened there?

A German U-boat torpedoed a ship called *City of Benares*, which had ninety CORB children aboard. It was hard to get everyone into the lifeboats safely due to rough seas and bad weather. Only thirteen children survived. They were discovered freezing and clinging to lifeboats in the North Atlantic Ocean.

Did the evacuations continue after that?

The British government decided that it was too dangerous to send any more children by ship after *City of Benares* was sunk. They also felt that the tide of the war was turning, and that Britain would survive the war. The Germans had begun to fight the Soviets, and there were fewer bombings of British cities.

How did the evacuated children feel when they came back home to Britain after the war?

Some of the children found it hard to go back home after spending years in a different country with a different family. They'd grown used to life in Canada or Australia, and they had become attached to their host families. Many children stayed in touch with their host families after the war. Some children found the long separation from their families so difficult that they never got over their homesickness.

Coming next in the
Canadian Flyer Adventures Series...

Canadian Flyer Adventures
#12

On
the Case

Emily and Matt visit the Wild West. Can they
help Mountie Sam Steele's murder investigation?

Visit
www.mapletreepress.com/canadianflyeradventures
for a sneak peek at the latest book in the series.

The *Canadian Flyer Adventures* Series

#1 Beware, Pirates!

#2 Danger, Dinosaurs!

#3 Crazy for Gold

#4 Yikes, Vikings!

#5 Flying High!

#6 Pioneer Kids

#7 Hurry, Freedom

#8 A Whale Tale

#9 All Aboard!

#10 Lost in the Snow

#11 Far from Home

Upcoming Book

Look out for the next book that will take
Emily and Matt on a new adventure:

#12 On the Case

And more to come!

More Praise for the Series

"[Emily and Matt] learn more than they ever could have from a history textbook. Every book in this new series promises to shed light on a different chapter of Canadian history."
~ *Montreal Gazette*

"Readers are in for a great adventure."
~ *Edmonton's Child*

"This series makes Canadian history fun, exciting and accessible."
~ *Chronicle Herald (Halifax)*

"[An] enthralling series for junior-school readers."
~ *Hamilton Spectator*

"...highly entertaining, very educational but not too challenging. A terrific new series."
~ *Resource Links*

"This wonderful new Canadian historical adventure series combines magic and history to whisk young readers away on adventure...A fun way to learn about Canada's past."
~ *BC Parent*

"Highly recommended."
~ *CM: Canadian Review of Materials*

Teacher Resource Guides now available online.
Please visit our website at
www.mapletreepress.com/canadianflyeradventures
to download tips and ideas for
using the series in the classroom.

About the Author

Frieda Wishinsky, a former teacher, is an award-winning picture- and chapter-book author, who has written many beloved and bestselling books for children. Frieda enjoys using humour and history in her work, while exploring new ways to tell a story. Her books have earned much critical praise, including a nomination for a Governor General's Award in 1999. In addition to the books in the *Canadian Flyer Adventures* series, Frieda has published *What's the Matter with Albert?*, *A Quest in Time*, and *Manya's Dream* with Maple Tree Press. Frieda lives in Toronto.

About the Illustrator

Leanne Franson has drawn as long as she can remember, and even before! She drew in her school notebooks, on scrap paper, on the sidewalk. And she read and read, especially stories that took place in the past, or had children who travelled to other and distant worlds. Leanne has lent her pencil and brush to over 80 books, and is happy to be accompanying Matt and Emily back into history in the *Canadian Flyer Adventures* series. Leanne works at home in Montreal, where she lives with her son Benjamin Taotao, her Saint Bernard, Gretchen, and two cats.